BEAVERS
CONSTRUCTION EXPERTS

KATIE LAJINESS

Big Buddy Books
An Imprint of Abdo Publishing
abdopublishing.com

AWESOME ANIMAL POWERS

abdopublishing.com

Published by Abdo Publishing, a division of ABDO, PO Box 398166, Minneapolis, Minnesota 55439. Copyright © 2019 by Abdo Consulting Group, Inc. International copyrights reserved in all countries. No part of this book may be reproduced in any form without written permission from the publisher. Big Buddy Books™ is a trademark and logo of Abdo Publishing.

Printed in the United States of America, North Mankato, Minnesota.
052018
092018

THIS BOOK CONTAINS RECYCLED MATERIALS

Cover Photo: mink/Getty Images.
Interior Photos: Ammit Jack/Shutterstock (p. 29); Anna39/Getty Images (p. 7); Bryant Aardema – bryants wildlife images/Getty Images (p. 19); Chase Dekker Wild-Live Images/Getty Images (p. 5); DonKurto/Getty Images (p. 17); DoucetPh/Getty Images (p. 23); Edwin Butter/Shutterstock (p. 27); Jeff R Clow/Getty Images (p. 9); jeffhochstrasser/Getty Images (p. 21); John Webster/Getty Images (p. 11); mink/Getty Images (p. 30); Robert McGouey / Wildlife/Alamy Stock Photo (p. 25); stanley45/Getty Images (p. 15).

Coordinating Series Editor: Tamara L. Britton
Contributing Editor: Jill Roesler
Graphic Design: Jenny Christensen, Erika Weldon

Library of Congress Control Number: 2017961415

Publisher's Cataloging-in-Publication Data

Names: Lajiness, Katie, author.
Title: Beavers: Construction experts / by Katie Lajiness.
Other titles: Construction experts
Description: Minneapolis, Minnesota : Abdo Publishing, 2019. | Series: Awesome animal powers | Includes online resources and index.
Identifiers: ISBN 9781532114960 (lib.bdg.) | ISBN 9781532155680 (ebook)
Subjects: LCSH: Beavers--Juvenile literature. | Beavers--Behavior--Juvenile literature. | Aquatic animals--Behavior--Juvenile literature. | Construction--Juvenile literature.
Classification: DDC 599.37--dc23

CONTENTS

THE BEAVER 4
BOLD BODIES 6
THAT'S AWESOME! 8
WHERE IN THE WORLD? 12
DAILY LIFE 14
A BEAVER'S LIFE 18
FAVORITE FOODS 22
BIRTH 24
DEVELOPMENT 26
FUTURE 28
FAST FACTS 30
GLOSSARY 31
ONLINE RESOURCES 31
INDEX 32

THE BEAVER

The world is full of awesome, powerful animals. Beavers (BEE-vuhrs) live in wetlands throughout North and South America, Asia, and Europe.

Beavers are construction **experts**. They use their large teeth to chew on wood. Then they use the wood to build underwater dams.

DID YOU KNOW?
Beavers greet each other by nipping at the other's cheeks.

Beavers are the largest rodents in North America. They are in the same family as squirrels and mice.

BOLD BODIES

Beavers have amazing bodies. Their webbed back feet make them great swimmers. Strong claws on their front feet help them dig deep holes. And thick fur keeps them warm and dry, even underwater.

These rodents can grow to be up to four feet (1 m) long. They weigh between 30 and 60 pounds (14 to 27 kg).

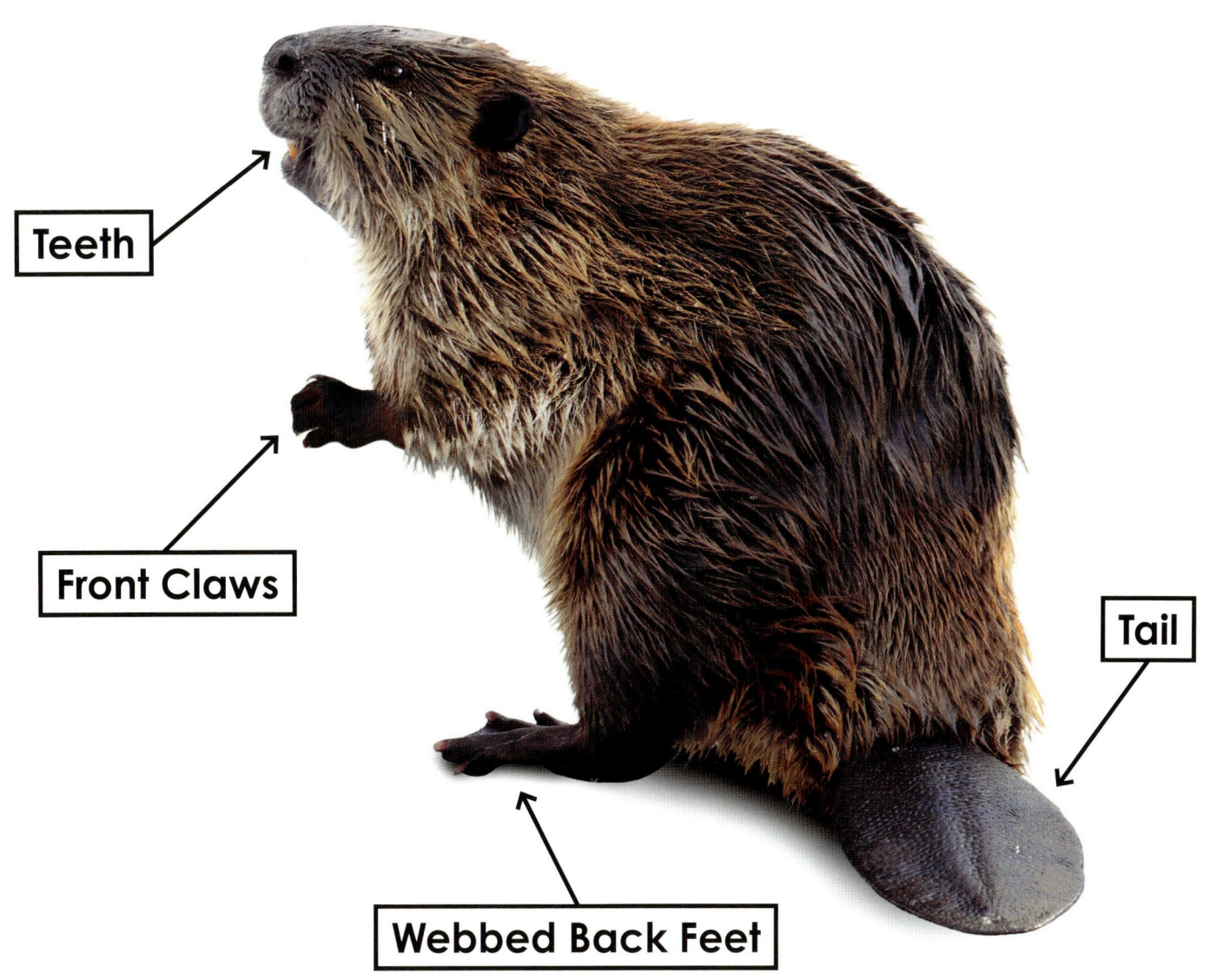

THAT'S AWESOME!

Beavers are great builders. They knock down trees by chewing through the trunks. Then they use branches, logs, plants, stones, and mud to build a dam.

DID YOU KNOW?
The world's largest beaver dam is in Alberta, Canada.

Beavers' front teeth grow throughout their lives. So, they chew on wood to keep their teeth from getting too long.

Dams block the flow of a stream. On one side, the stream becomes a pond about six feet (2 m) deep.

Beavers pile sticks and logs to create a mound in the pond. On top of the mound, they build a **lodge**. That is where beaver families live.

The lodge is where beavers rest, stay warm, and care for their kits.

WHERE IN THE

Beavers live in streams, rivers, **marshes**, and ponds. They mostly live in North America and Europe. But some are found in the southern tip of South America. Others live in western and eastern Asia.

DAILY LIFE

Beavers spend their time eating, **grooming**, sleeping, or building. They gnaw on trees for food and to build dams. The beavers chew away at the trunk until the tree falls.

Beavers can chew through a six-inch (15 cm) tree in 15 minutes. Each year, one beaver can chew through hundreds of trees.

Beavers sleep in **lodges** all day. As the sun sets, beavers leave their lodges to eat. They stay out all night building new dams and searching for food.

If a **predator** appears, beavers slap their tails on the water. The sound tells other beavers to hide or quickly swim away.

Beavers are less active during colder months. But they do not sleep through the entire winter.

A BEAVER'S LIFE

Beaver **lodges** usually have two exits. One leads to the pond. The other could lead to dry land.

They store food at the bottom of their ponds. This way, beavers can reach their food without being seen by **predators**. They spend spring and summer adding food to the underwater pile.

Beavers can swim underwater for about 15 minutes without coming up for air.

In the winter, beavers spend most of their time in their **lodges**. When it gets cold, the surface of the pond freezes. The beavers swim under the ice to reach their food pile. This way, they don't have to go outside to search for food.

Beavers can tuck their cheeks behind their front teeth. This keeps water out of their mouths while carrying wood underwater.

FAVORITE FOODS

Although they have strong teeth and jaws, beavers do not eat other animals. Instead, they eat plants. Tree bark, roots, and leaves are some of their favorites. They also enjoy eating twigs, berries, and cattails.

Beavers have favorite foods. They prefer the bark and twigs from aspen trees!

BIRTH

Beavers **mate** for life. A female beaver is **pregnant** for about four months. Then she gives birth to one to six babies called kits. Each kit weighs less than a pound (0.5 kg).

Beaver kits can swim 24 hours after birth!

DEVELOPMENT

These animals live in groups with four to 12 members. The groups include parents and kits from the past two **breeding** seasons. Beavers usually live between five and ten years. But some can live up to 24 years.

Kits stay in or near the lodge for their first two weeks.

FUTURE

As time passes, rivers, lakes, and wetlands continue to change or dry up. This means that the beavers' natural **habitats** are under **threat**.

But today, many groups work hard to help beavers stay safe and happy. So beavers will continue building their dams and **lodges** for many years!

Long ago, humans hunted almost all the beavers in North America and Europe. But today, the number of beavers is back to normal.

FAST FACTS

ANIMAL TYPE: Rodent

SIZE: Up to four feet (1 m) long

WEIGHT: Between 30 and 60 pounds (14 to 27 kg)

HABITAT: Streams, rivers, marshes, ponds, and lakeshores

DIET: Plants such as tree bark, roots, leaves, twigs, berries, and cattails

AWESOME ANIMAL POWER: Beavers are construction experts that are second only to humans in their ability to change the environment.

GLOSSARY

breed a group of animals sharing the same appearance and features.

expert showing special skill or knowledge gained from experience or training.

groom to clean and care for.

habitat a place where a living thing is naturally found.

lodge a den or resting place of an animal.

marsh an area of low, wet land.

mate to join as a couple in order to reproduce, or have babies.

predator a person or animal that hunts and kills animals for food.

pregnant having one or more babies growing within the body.

threat something that could be harmful.

To learn more about beavers, visit **abdobooklinks.com**. These links are routinely monitored and updated to provide the most current information available.

INDEX

Asia **4, 12**

behavior **4, 5, 6, 8, 9, 10, 11, 14, 15, 16, 17, 18, 19, 20, 21, 26, 28, 30**

birth **24, 25, 27**

Canada **9**

climate **28**

communication **5, 16**

conservation **28, 29**

development **9, 11, 24, 25, 26, 27**

Europe **4, 12, 29**

food **4, 10, 12, 18, 20, 28, 30**

habitat **4, 8, 9, 10, 11, 20**

homes **4, 8, 9, 10, 11, 14, 16, 18, 20**

life span **26**

mating **24**

North America **4, 5, 12, 29**

physical characteristics **4, 5, 6, 7, 9, 16, 21, 22, 24, 30**

predators **16, 18**

rodents **5, 30**

South America **4, 12**